Her Halloween Happiness

A SMALL TOWN HOLIDAY SWEET ROMANCE

SWEPT AWAY IN BUTTERCUP BAY
BOOK FOUR

MOLLY ARDEN

Copyright © 2024 Molly Arden

All rights reserved.

No portion of this book may be reproduced in any form without permission from the publisher, except as permitted by U.S. copyright law.

Exceptions: Reviewers may quote brief passages for reviews.

This is a work of fiction. Names, characters, places, and incidents either are the product of the author's imagination or are used fictitiously. Any resemblance to actual persons, living or dead, events, or locales is entirely coincidental.

Contents

CHAPTER 1

Scarlett

I **STEP** out of my car and take a deep breath, letting the crisp autumn air of Buttercup Bay wash over me. The smell of pine and a hint of woodsmoke linger in the breeze, curling through the streets and slipping into my lungs like the promise of something good. It's the kind of air that feels clean, that makes you feel like you've left all the noise and chaos behind—exactly what I need after the whirlwind that was my life in the city.

As I take in my surroundings, I can't help but smile. The town is everything I'd imagined: small, cozy, and full of charm. The square is lined with narrow streets where cozy shops sit nestled against each other like old friends. The stone walkways glisten under the afternoon sun, and groups of people pass by, smiling and waving as if they've known me forever. The warmth here is palpable, even as autumn's chill drapes itself over the landscape. It feels like a storybook—a place where new beginnings might actually stick.

I grab my bag from the passenger seat and head toward The Lit Lantern, my new bookstore and the cornerstone of my fresh start. It still feels surreal—owning a shop like this. My fingers trail along the edge of the wooden door as I unlock it, and when I step inside, a familiar sense of calm wraps around me. The smell of old books mingles with the faintest hint of vanilla from the candle I lit last night before closing. The shelves stretch up toward the ceiling, packed with spines in every color, shape, and size. Some of them are old friends; others are waiting to be discovered.

I walk behind the counter and pull out my calendar, flipping through the pages to the end of October. The Halloween Bash is fast approaching—my first big event as a business owner, and the pressure to make it memorable is already gnawing at me. I've been planning a haunted history tour to weave through the town's streets, a mix of spooky legends and local folklore. The tour will end here with a ghostly reading night in the bookstore. It'll be perfect—if I can find the right story to tie it all together.

But I need something real. Something local. Something that will make the town feel like it's a part of the story.

The bell above the door jingles cheerily, pulling me out of my swirling thoughts and momentarily grounding me in the present. Martha Greene strides in, her presence brightening the room as she carries a basket brimming with freshly baked cinnamon scones, their warm, sweet aroma wafting through the air. She's been my first real friend since moving to this town, always popping in unannounced with delightful treats or the latest gossip from the bakery next door, her enthusiasm infectious and her laughter a welcome sound in the quiet bookstore.

"Good morning, darling!" Martha's voice rings out with a warmth that rivals the comforting scent of cinnamon wafting in behind her. "I brought you some sustenance for the day ahead. You're going to need it with the Halloween Bash coming up." Her eyes sparkle with excitement as if the very thought of the upcoming festivities energizes her.

I smile, feeling a wave of gratitude wash over me for her cheerful presence. "You're a lifesaver. Honestly, I'm starting to feel a little overwhelmed." The thought of organizing the event looms large in my mind, but her support makes the task seem less daunting.

Martha sets the basket down on the counter with a flourish, the scones nestled inside like little treasures, and gives me a look that blends amusement with a healthy dose of encouragement. "You'll be fine. The town is buzzing about the tour you're putting together." Her faith in me is a balm for my nerves, and I can't help but feel a flicker of excitement at the prospect of bringing the community together for such a spirited occasion.

"Well, I still need the right story to make it special," I admit, pouring us both a cup of rich, aromatic coffee from the thermos I keep behind the counter. The steam rises gently, filling the air with a comforting warmth. "I was thinking… there must be some local legend I can use. Something spooky but real."

Martha's cheerful expression falters, just for a second, as if a shadow has crossed her face. She hesitates, stirring her coffee absentmindedly, the spoon clinking softly against the ceramic mug. "There is one story," she says quietly, her voice barely above a whisper. "But I'm not sure it's one the town likes to talk about."

I lean in closer, intrigued, my curiosity piqued by her sudden seriousness. "What is it?" I ask, eager to uncover whatever mystery she's holding back.

Martha lowers her voice even further, glancing toward the window as if she fears someone might overhear our conversation. "There's a family. Have you heard of them?" Her tone carries a weight, hinting at a tale steeped in both intrigue and discomfort.

I shake my head. The name is unfamiliar to me, yet it feels like the beginning of something significant.

She sighs, her tone taking on a more conspiratorial note. "Wade Grayson lives up in the mountains, far away from everyone. He's the last of his family. Rugged, quiet, and, well… devastatingly handsome, if you ask the women in town. But he keeps to himself after what happened with his fiancée."

"What happened?" I ask, my curiosity piqued, eager to unravel the mystery shrouding this enigmatic figure.

Martha's eyes flick back to me, a flicker of something—sympathy or perhaps fear—passing through them. "An accident. They say he blames himself for what happened that day, the weight of grief heavier than any mountain. After that, Wade shut himself off from the world, retreating into the shadows of his family's legacy. No one really sees him anymore, except when he makes the occasional trip into town for supplies, his presence a fleeting whisper in the bustling market."

I blink, taking in her words, feeling the weight of the tragedy settle in my chest. "That's… tragic," I manage to say, my mind racing with the implications of such loss.

Martha nods, her expression grave. "It is. But his family has been part of the town for generations, woven into its very fabric. Some folks say the Graysons are cursed—every few decades, something terrible happens to someone in the family, as if fate has it out for them. The town's old-timers love gathering around the campfire to share chilling stories about it; each tale laced with a blend of fascination and dread. But Wade? He's not interested in entertaining old ghosts; he prefers the solitude of his mountain home, where the echoes of the past can't reach him."

The image of Wade Grayson—this mysterious man in the mountains—begins to take shape in my mind. Rugged, quiet, haunted by loss. I can almost see him standing in the shadows, watching the town from afar, keeping his pain tucked away from prying eyes.

Martha pats my hand. "I don't know if Wade would appreciate you digging into his family's past, but if you want a real ghost story, the Graysons are about as real as it gets."

I nod slowly, my thoughts swirling like leaves caught in a gentle breeze. "Thanks, Martha. I'll think about it."

She smiles brightly, her expression warm and encouraging, before making her way to the door, leaving behind the comforting aroma of cinnamon and the inviting warmth of her presence. But my mind drifts away from the delectable scones, now fixated on Wade Grayson. There's an undeniable pull toward him—something about his presence lingers in the air, a mystery that beckons me to unravel it. He feels like the key to unlocking not just my event but perhaps even deeper truths hidden within this town.

I steal a glance out the window, my gaze wandering to the distant mountains shrouded in mist. A man like him… he's a puzzle, intricate and layered, and I've always had a knack for piecing together such enigmas. The thrill of the chase ignites a spark within me, urging me to delve deeper into his story.

CHAPTER 2

Wade

THE CABIN IS QUIET, save for the soft rustling of leaves outside. I wake to the familiar sounds of the forest—birds chirping, branches swaying in the breeze, the distant creak of trees stretching their limbs. I sit up in bed, the morning light filtering through the cracks in the wooden walls. It's peaceful here. Still. That's the way I like it. The mountain is far removed from the bustle of Buttercup Bay, and most days, I don't have to talk to anyone. It's better that way. Less messy.

I roll out of bed, the cold wooden floor creaking beneath my feet as I head to the window. From here, I can see the slope of the mountain, the trees sprawling out into a vast sea of green and gold. The leaves are starting to turn, autumn creeping in with its cool, crisp air. The change in the seasons has always been my favorite—especially since I came here, alone, after… after Charlotte.

I swallow the familiar knot that forms in my throat at the thought of her. Five years, and it still feels like yesterday. The accident. The hike that went wrong. The way I couldn't save her. There's a part of me that stays frozen in that moment, still tangled in the guilt, still convinced that I should have done something—anything—to stop it from happening.

I shake my head, pushing the thoughts away, and pull on my flannel shirt and worn jeans. There's no use digging up the past. I chose this life—up here, away from the town, from people—because it's all I deserve. Solitude. Quiet. And if that means my days are spent chopping wood, hunting for my meals, and carving pieces of scrap wood into something useful or beautiful, then so be it. It's enough. At least, that's what I keep telling myself.

I grab my jacket and step outside, breathing in the sharp, cool air. Today, I need to go down into town for supplies. I've been putting it off for as long as I could, but there are some things you can't get in the wild—soap, batteries, coffee. The essentials. I hate going down there. It always feels like people are watching, wondering what happened to me. The truth is, they probably are. I've become the town's mystery man, the recluse. And maybe that's what I am now—someone who's better off keeping to himself.

I load up the old truck, my only link to the life I left behind. It grumbles to life, the engine groaning as I pull onto the dirt road that leads down the mountain. The familiar rumble of the tires on gravel keeps my mind occupied as the trees whip past the windows. The farther I get from my cabin, the tighter the knot in my stomach grows. It's not fear. Not really. It's the weight of having to interact, having to engage with people who look at me and see only what I've lost.

As I round a bend in the road, something catches my eye—a car pulled off to the side, steam pouring from under the hood. I slow down, instinct taking over before I even have a chance to think. My eyes narrow as I scan the scene. There's a woman standing next to the car, hands on her hips, her hair like fire against the autumn backdrop. She's pacing, looking down at the engine like it might answer her if she stares hard enough.

I should keep driving. It's not my problem. Someone else will come along. But something makes me stop. Maybe it's the way she's standing, shoulders tense but determined, or maybe it's that flash of red hair that I can't ignore. Either way, I pull over and cut the engine.

As I step out of the truck, the brisk autumn air hits my face, invigorating and crisp, prompting me to shove my hands deep into my jacket pockets. I walk slowly toward her, taking in the scene—the way she stands there, a vivid splash of color against the dullness of the roadside. She turns when she hears my footsteps, her eyes bright with a mixture of relief and frustration, like a storm cloud battling against a sunset.

"Thank God," she exclaims, her smile a beacon despite the tension in the air. Her voice is warm, a comforting contrast to the chill around us, even though her situation clearly isn't. "I thought I was going to be stuck here for hours, just me and this stubborn hunk of metal."

I nod, keeping my distance, sensing the weight of her predicament. "What happened?"

"I don't know," she replies, exasperation tinging her words. "One minute, everything was fine, and the next, it's smoking like it's on fire." She gestures toward the hood with a sweeping motion, blowing a rebellious strand of hair out of her face, revealing the determined set of her jaw. "Do you know anything about cars?"

"Enough," I say, stepping closer, cautious but undeniably curious. She's not from around here; I'd remember if I'd seen her before. She's… different. Too bright for a place like this, with its muted colors and worn-out scenery. Too full of life, like a flickering flame in the midst of a gathering dusk. "I'm Wade. Wade Grayson."

I pop the hood, and a wave of heat and steam escapes, swirling around me like a ghostly shroud as I peer into the chaotic mess beneath. I can sense her gaze fixed on me, a mix of curiosity and anticipation, but I keep my attention firmly on the engine. It's easier that way—easier to maintain a sense of detachment from the moment, from her.

"Thank you for stopping," she says after a brief silence, her voice breaking through the tension. "I'm Scarlett, by the way. I just moved to town a few months ago—opened up the bookstore on

Main Street." Her words carry an infectious enthusiasm as if she's sharing a secret about a hidden treasure.

I grunt in acknowledgment, nodding slightly but keeping my responses clipped and to the point. "You from the city?"

"Yeah," she replies, her smile brightening again, illuminating the space around us. "It's been an adjustment, but I'm loving it here. The air is cleaner; and people are friendlier. It's like living in a different world." There's a wistfulness in her voice as if she's still marveling at the novelty of it all, and I can't help but wonder what led her to this sleepy place.

I don't respond to that. I don't have much to say about friendly people. But I can't help but notice how easily she talks, how natural it is for her. She fills the silence, but not in a way that feels forced. She's warm, vibrant—everything I'm not.

"Are you coming to the Halloween Bash?" she asks, her tone light and casual as if she's inviting me to a simple afternoon picnic rather than an event steeped in ghostly tales. "I'm planning a haunted history tour. It's going to be fun—spooky stories, local legends… you should come. It'll be a great way to get to know the town better."

I tighten a bolt under the hood, my hands working reflexively while I keep my gaze fixed on the engine, as if the mechanics might somehow shield me from her enthusiasm. "I don't do town events," I reply, my voice lacking any hint of warmth.

She chuckles, clearly undeterred by my gruff response, her laughter ringing like a cheerful bell in the cool air. "Well, if you change your mind, you know where to find me." The lightness in her voice suggests she believes I might reconsider, and I can't help but admire her optimism.

I steal a brief glance at her, and she's smiling, bright and open, radiating a warmth that feels almost foreign to me. It makes something stir in my chest, a flicker of emotion I haven't felt in a long time. Something like interest. Or maybe danger, a warning that this connection could lead to something unexpected. I'm not sure which one it is, but I can't shake the feeling.

Once the engine's fixed, I straighten up, wiping my hands on my jeans, the grease smudging against the fabric. "Try it now," I say, gesturing for her to give it another go.

Scarlett hops into the driver's seat with an eagerness that's infectious. She turns the key, and the engine roars to life, a powerful sound that fills the air with renewed energy. Her face lights up like it's Christmas morning, joy spilling from her in waves. "Thank you! Seriously, I owe you one," she exclaims, her excitement palpable.

I nod, already stepping back to give her space, the corners of my mouth twitching upward despite my attempts to remain nonchalant. "It's nothing," I reply, brushing off her gratitude as I focus on the mechanics.

"Still," she insists, her voice warm as she gets out of the car and stands in front of me, her eyes sparkling with sincerity. "I really appreciate it. If you're ever near the bookstore, come by. First coffee's on me." Her offer hangs in the air, a tempting invitation that feels both casual and loaded with potential.

Her offer hangs in the air between us, but I don't respond. I just nod again, retreating to my truck. Before I can stop myself, I glance back at her one last time. She's watching me, her eyes filled with curiosity. And something else. Something I can't let myself think about.

As I pull back onto the road, leaving her behind, I feel that strange stir in my chest again. A pull. A spark. I shake it off. She's not for me. Someone like Scarlett doesn't belong in my world.

And the last thing I need is to let someone like her in.

CHAPTER 3

Scarlett

BACK AT THE BOOKSTORE, I can't stop thinking about Wade Grayson. The image of him standing beside my car, his hands steady as he worked on the engine, his quiet presence, stays with me. There was something about him—something heavy, like a shadow he carries around with him. Dark but compelling. It's hard to explain. Most people wear their emotions in a way that's easy to read, but Wade... he's different. Closed off. Guarded.

And yet, even with the few words we exchanged, I felt something. A weight, yes, but also a kind of strength, like the world hadn't been kind to him, but he stood firm anyway. I shake my head, trying to push the thought away. I barely know the man. But it's hard to ignore the way my curiosity pulls at me like a string tied around my chest. What happened to him? Why does he seem like someone who's hiding from the world?

The soft creak of the bookstore floor beneath my feet grounds me as I glance around the shop. I need to focus. The Halloween Bash is just around the corner, and there's too much to do for me to be daydreaming about the town's mysterious recluse. The store smells like the vanilla candle I lit earlier, mingling with the scent of old books—a combination that usually calms me. But today, my mind is all over the place.

I glance at my checklist on the counter. Decorations, check. Flyers, check. Now, I just need the story that'll anchor the haunted history tour. I jot down a few ideas, but my pen hovers over the paper. Somehow, none of these ideas seem good enough. What this event needs is a real story—one the town knows, one that will feel personal to the people who live here. Something that will tie everything together.

The bell above the door jingles, and I look up to see Martha, her basket of cinnamon scones in hand and a wide smile on her face. She's become my rock since I moved to Buttercup Bay, always popping in with baked goods or local gossip. Today is no different.

"Morning, darling!" she calls out cheerfully, setting the basket down on the counter with a gentle thud. The rich, inviting aroma of cinnamon wafts through the air instantly, wrapping around me like a warm hug. "How's the Halloween planning going?"

I let out a heavy sigh, but I manage to offer her a bright smile as I pour us both steaming cups of coffee from the thermos nestled behind the counter. "It's... coming together, slowly but surely. I'm still grappling with finding the right story for the haunted tour that will truly resonate."

Martha raises an intrigued eyebrow, her fingers delicately plucking a scone from the basket. "What kind of story are you thinking?" she asks, curiosity lacing her voice as she leans in, eager to hear more.

"I want something real," I say, handing her a cup. "Something that'll make people feel connected to the town's history. Spooky, but not too far-fetched. The problem is, I can't think of any good local legends that capture the essence of what we're trying to do here."

Martha hesitates, her hand stopping mid-reach for the sugar. It's such a subtle gesture that I almost miss it, but the shift in her demeanor piques my curiosity. "Well," she begins slowly, her voice tinged with hesitation, "there's one story, but it's... not exactly the kind people like to talk about."

I tilt my head, intrigued, eager to uncover whatever hidden tale she might have. "What is it?"

She glances around the shop, her eyes darting as if to ensure that the walls themselves won't betray our conversation, even though we're alone in the cozy little café. Then, lowering her voice to a near whisper, she leans in closer. "The Grayson family. I was telling you about it the other day."

A flicker of recognition sparks within me, igniting memories I didn't realize were there. "Wade Grayson?" The man who'd just fixed my car flashes in my mind, his stormy gray eyes piercing through the dim light of the café, and I recall the tension that seemed to coil beneath his calm exterior, hinting at deeper stories waiting to be unearthed.

Martha nods. "He's the last of the Grayson line. His family's been here for generations, and there's a lot of history tied to them. But it's not a happy one." She stirs her coffee absentmindedly. "Wade lost his fiancée, Charlotte, in a hiking accident up in the mountains about five years ago. They say he's never forgiven himself for it."

My heart tightens. "I remember you said something about an accident. What happened, exactly?"

"She fell. The trail was slick from the rain, and it was one of those freak accidents. But Wade... he blames himself. He was the one leading the hike. After she died, he just... disappeared. Shut himself off from everyone and moved up into the mountains. You probably noticed how he is—quiet, distant. He barely comes into town anymore."

The weight of her words sinks in, and suddenly, Wade's aloofness makes a little more sense. I think about the way he looked at me, the way he kept his distance even as he helped. A man carrying that kind of guilt... no wonder he keeps the world at arm's length.

I take a sip of coffee, the warmth doing little to ease the sudden tightness in my chest. "That's... awful. I had no idea."

Martha's eyes soften as she watches me. "He's been through a lot. But if anyone could tell you a real ghost story, it'd be Wade. The Grayson family has had their fair share of tragedy over the years, and some folks say they're cursed. Of course, that's just town gossip, but... who knows?"

I nod slowly, my thoughts swirling like a tempest in a teacup. Wade's story is more than just idle gossip; it's raw, visceral, and profoundly real. It could very well be the key to making this event truly meaningful, transforming it from a mere gathering into something with depth and resonance. But beyond that, I can't shake the pang of empathy that wells up inside me for him. He's hiding from the world, burying himself in solitude, much like I once tried to bury my own heartbreak when Gavin made the choice to prioritize his career over our relationship.

The memory of Gavin creeps up on me, uninvited, like a shadow lurking just out of sight. I hadn't thought about him much since I moved here, convinced that I'd put that chapter behind me. Yet, suddenly, the feelings rush back with a vengeance— the disappointment, the hurt that I thought had faded into the background. We'd been together for years, woven into each other's lives, and I had genuinely believed we would build a future together.

But when the moment of truth arrived, he chose his career. He always insisted that I deserved more than what he could offer, but in my heart, it felt like a convenient excuse to push me away. His departure left me grappling with a profound sense of betrayal, questioning whether I could ever trust anyone again, whether love could ever be safe.

Now, as I sit here, lost in thought about Wade, a whirlwind of emotions washes over me. I wonder if he feels the same weight of grief pressing down on him. Is he also trapped, afraid to let anyone in, just like I am? Perhaps, like me, he's simply waiting for a sign, for someone to guide him toward the realization that it's okay to move on from the shadows of our past.

But I can't dwell on that now. The Halloween Bash is approaching with alarming speed, and I need to concentrate on the preparations. Still, Wade's presence clings to my thoughts, a haunting enigma I can't quite decipher, like a puzzle with missing pieces that refuse to fit together.

"I think I might need his help," I say after a moment, the thought surprising even me as it spills from my lips. "For the haunted tour. If anyone knows the town's history—especially the Graysons

—it's him." The words resonate with a strange kind of clarity, igniting a flicker of hope within me.

Martha's eyes widen slightly, a mixture of surprise and intrigue dancing across her face, but she doesn't seem entirely taken aback. "You're brave, darling. Most folks wouldn't even think about asking him. But... maybe it's exactly what he needs. A chance to reconnect, to step back into the light." Her words linger in the air, an invitation to consider possibilities I hadn't dared to entertain before.

I smile at her, though my mind is already racing. Wade Grayson might just be the missing piece to my event. And maybe... maybe something more.

As Martha leaves, I glance out the window toward the distant mountains. Wade is up there, alone, carrying the weight of his past like a cloak. I can't explain it, but I feel like I need to understand him. Not just for the tour. For something deeper.

I take a deep breath and make a decision. Tomorrow, I'll go find him. If anyone can tell the story of Buttercup Bay's ghosts, it's Wade Grayson.

THE CABIN IS SILENT, save for the steady crackle of the fire in the hearth. I've always appreciated the quiet up here. It gives me space to think, to breathe, without anyone trying to pull me into conversations I don't want to have or asking questions I don't want to answer. The world doesn't intrude on me here, and I like it that way. At least, I usually do.

Today, though, the quiet feels different. It's restless, almost. The image of Scarlett—her bright red hair against the autumn trees, the warmth in her voice—keeps creeping into my mind, even though I tell myself I shouldn't be thinking about her. She doesn't belong in my world, and I don't belong in hers.

I drop into the chair by the fireplace, running my hands over my face. I shouldn't have stopped to help her. It would've been easier to keep driving, to let someone else deal with it. But something made me stop. That curiosity—her smile, her ease in conversation—sticks with me like a burr I can't shake off.

I try to focus on something else, so I reach for the wood and carving tools beside me. My hands know this work by heart. I pick up the knife and start carving into the soft wood, letting the repetition calm my mind. The firelight flickers over the smooth surface as I shape the figure with practiced ease. Usually, I don't think too much about what I'm making—I just carve until something takes form. It's like the wood tells me what it wants to be.

Today, though, something different happens. As I keep carving, I realize I've been shaping the features of a woman—soft lines, flowing hair—and before I even know it, I see her. Scarlett. Her face takes form under my hands, and for a moment, I just stare, shocked. How did that happen? How could I have been thinking about her enough to do this without even realizing it?

I set the carving down quickly, like it might burn me if I hold on any longer. A tight knot forms in my chest, that familiar weight of guilt pressing down. This is wrong. I shouldn't be thinking about anyone like that. Not since Charlotte.

Charlotte's face flashes in my mind, just as vivid as it was the day she died. That smile of hers—God, I loved her smile. It lit up the room and warmed my heart; I thought I'd spend my life with her, sharing dreams and laughter. But then she was gone in an instant, leaving behind an echo of joy that turned into nothing but regret. I swore, after she died, that I'd never let myself feel that kind of loss again. And I've kept that promise—until now. Until Scarlett.

The guilt twists like a knife, sharp and unyielding. What right do I have to feel anything for anyone else? How could I even entertain the thought of moving on when Charlotte's memory still haunts me every single day, a ghost that refuses to be exorcised from my heart?

I push the carving to the side, the motion abrupt and almost frantic. I need to get out of here. Being alone with my thoughts is too much right now, an unbearable weight pressing down on me. I grab my jacket, the fabric cool against my fingertips, and head for the door, deciding to go into town for supplies. Maybe the drive will clear my head, allow me to breathe again, and offer a momentary escape from the turmoil within.

THE TOWN IS BUSTLING when I arrive, as it usually is at this time of day, a lively blend of voices and laughter spilling out from the cafes and shops. I keep my head down, focusing on the pavement as I park and make my way toward the store, trying to blend in with the crowd. I don't need much—just a few essentials to get me through the week. I'm in and out quickly, moving with purpose and not lingering any longer than I have to. The last thing I want is to make small talk with anyone, to engage in the trivial banter that feels so foreign to me right now.

But as I turn the corner, heading back to my truck, I see her. Scarlett. She's standing by the bakery, her laughter mingling with the sweet aroma of fresh pastries, talking with Martha, her hands gesturing animatedly as she discusses something that seems to ignite her spirit. Probably her event, I think, recalling the buzz around town about it. Even from a distance, I can see the energy radiating off her—she's the kind of person who lights up a room just by being in it, her presence vibrant and magnetic.

I stop for a moment, rooted in place, watching her. There's something enchanting about her, the way she seems so effortlessly at ease with people, how she draws them in with her warmth and genuine laughter. She's so... alive. It stirs something deep within me, something I haven't felt in a long time. That pull. That flicker of desire that flares up like a spark in the darkness. But just as quickly as it comes, it's drowned out by the familiar ache of loss that washes over me like a cold wave. What am I doing? What business do I have standing here, watching her like this, when I should be moving on?

I turn to leave, hoping to slip away unnoticed, but I'm too late to escape her keen awareness.

"Wade!" Her voice rings out, bright and full of life, just like the rest of her. It dances through the air, pulling me back as I reluctantly turn to face her, my heart betraying me with an unwelcome flutter. She hurries over, her steps light and eager, as if she's been waiting for this moment.

"Hey," she says, a little out of breath, her smile wide and infectious, lighting up the space around us. "I was hoping I'd see you again."

I nod, trying to keep my face as neutral as possible, a mask that hides the turmoil brewing beneath the surface. "You doing okay? Car holding up?"

"Yep, all good, thanks to you," she replies, her eyes shining with gratitude and something else— something that makes it hard to breathe. "I actually wanted to talk to you about something if you have a minute."

I can already feel my defenses going up, a fortress rising around my heart, but I don't take a step back. "What's that?" My voice is steadier than I feel, but inside, a storm of uncertainty rages.

She glances around, lowering her voice slightly. "I'm putting together a haunted history tour for the Halloween Bash. You know, spooky stories, local legends. And, well... I was hoping you might be able to help. Your family has a lot of history in this town, and I thought maybe—"

"No." The word escapes my lips, sharper than I intended, and I catch the surprise flicker across her face, wide and unguarded.

I take a breath, attempting to rein in the sudden whirlwind of anger and guilt that flares up inside me, a tempest I thought I had learned to control. "I'm not interested in revisiting that. Not with anyone." The emphasis on "anyone" hangs in the air, thick with unspoken history.

She blinks, clearly taken aback by my abruptness, her expression shifting from curiosity to confusion. "I didn't mean to—"

"I know what you meant," I cut her off, my tone sharper than intended, feeling the familiar weight of the past pressing down on me like an anchor. "But it's not something I want to talk about. Ever." The finality in my words feels like a protective barrier, one I'm desperate to maintain.

A moment of silence stretches between us, heavy and charged. Her smile has faded, replaced by a look of disappointment that tugs at my heart, making it feel even heavier. She nods slowly, taking a step back, the distance a silent acknowledgment of my boundaries. "Okay. I understand. I didn't mean to push." Her voice is softer now, tinged with regret, and it lingers in the air like a fading echo.

I don't know what to say, so I just nod, muttering something that might have been an apology before I turn and walk away. The guilt follows me, creeping in like a shadow. I shouldn't have been so harsh with her. She didn't deserve that. But I can't—won't—dig up that part of my life again. Not for anyone.

As I head back to my truck, I glance over my shoulder once. Scarlett's still standing where I left her, watching me with a look I can't quite read. But I can't stop. I've spent years building these walls, and I'm not about to let someone like Scarlett tear them down.

CHAPTER 5

Scarlett

I'M STILL THINKING about the way Wade shut me down. The way his eyes hardened, his words clipped and cold. There was no room for argument, no softness in his voice when he said, *I'm not interested in revisiting that.* I told myself not to take it personally, that it's just him, but it's hard not to feel a sting of rejection.

Still, I can't shake the feeling that Wade isn't as closed off as he wants people to believe. He didn't walk away from me the moment we met. He could've driven past me when my car broke down, but he didn't. And then, when we talked, there was a flicker—something in his eyes that softened, like he was hesitating, second-guessing. That look stayed with me, nagging at the back of my mind, making me wonder if there's more to him than the walls he's built up around himself.

I've always been good at sensing when someone's holding back. And Wade? He's practically hiding behind those walls, retreating into a place where no one can reach him. But that doesn't stop me from wanting to try. I don't know why I'm so drawn to him, why I can't just let it go. Maybe because I've been hurt too, and I know what it's like to put up walls, to think that keeping people out will protect you. But it doesn't.

I glance out the window of The Lit Lantern, my gaze drifting up toward the mountains. I know what I need to do.

THE ROAD LEADING up the mountain is rough, the narrow path winding through dense trees that seem to grow closer together the higher I go. It's quieter up here, the hum of the town below fading into the distance, replaced by the occasional rustle of leaves and the soft call of birds. The farther I drive, the more I feel the weight of where I'm going—a place that belongs to Wade, a world he's built for himself far removed from everyone else.

By the time I reach his cabin, my heart races in my chest, each beat echoing my uncertainty. Maybe this is a bad idea, a thought that flits through my mind like a restless bird. I can't shake the fear that he might not be happy to see me, that he'll simply shut me out again, retreating into that wall he's built around himself. But I have to try; I need to talk to him, to find a way to break through whatever's holding him back.

I park the car on the gravel, the crunch of stones beneath the tires punctuating the stillness of the forest. Stepping out, I take a deep breath, inhaling the crisp, pine-scented air as I look around. His cabin is just as I imagined—sturdy and isolated, nestled within the thick embrace of the towering trees. It feels like it has been cut off from the rest of the world, a sanctuary where time drifts lazily, and the weight of old memories lingers in the air like a faint whisper. I hesitate for a moment, my hand hovering near the door before I summon the courage to walk toward the front entrance.

Just as I raise my hand to knock, the door swings open, and there he stands—Wade, framed in the doorway, his expression hard and unreadable. He doesn't look surprised to see me, but there's no hint of pleasure in his gaze either, just a guarded wariness that sends a chill through me.

"Scarlett," he says, his voice low and guarded, each word laced with an undercurrent of tension. "What are you doing here?"

I swallow hard, forcing myself to stand my ground despite the knot of anxiety twisting in my stomach. "I wanted to talk to you."

Wade raises an eyebrow, his expression a calculated mask of indifference, but he doesn't invite me in. His hand rests on the doorframe, a silent barrier, as if he's ready to slam the door shut if I push too far into this fragile moment. "About what?"

I take a deep breath, trying to keep my voice steady, even as my heart races. "About the haunted tour. I know you don't want to relive anything painful, and I'm not asking you to. But the town needs to hear the full story. Your family's story."

His eyes narrow slightly, muscles in his jaw tightening as if bracing for a blow. "I already told you I'm not interested."

"I know, and I respect that," I say quickly, trying to soften my tone, desperate to break through the wall he's constructed. "But I think you're the only one who can help me. You know the history better than anyone else in this town. You don't have to share anything personal—just the facts. That's all I'm asking." I let the words hang in the air, hoping he can sense the sincerity behind them, the urgency that fuels my request.

For a moment, there's nothing but silence between us. He doesn't move, doesn't speak, and I can feel the weight of his hesitation pressing down on both of us. I'm about to apologize, to tell him I'll leave, when he finally steps aside just enough to let me in.

"Come in," he mutters, though his voice is tight.

I nod, stepping inside his cabin. It's simple, but not in a bad way—more like everything here serves a purpose. The furniture is sturdy, the walls lined with bookshelves and a few scattered carvings. There's a fire crackling in the hearth, casting a soft glow over the room. It feels warm, but not welcoming. It feels like a place where someone hides from the world.

Wade strides over to the sturdy wooden table that occupies the center of the room, an unspoken invitation in his gesture for me to take a seat. I comply, forcing myself to focus on the surface of the table rather than the rapid thumping of my heart, which echoes in my ears as I absorb the details of my surroundings. I can't help but wonder how long it's been since anyone shared a meal or conversation at this table with him, how long he's been isolated in this carefully curated space.

He lowers himself into the chair directly opposite me, his expression inscrutable as his gaze locks onto mine, yet there's a distinct chill in the air, an unmistakable barrier that separates us. There's no warmth in his eyes, only a guarded distance that suggests he's not accustomed to sharing this part of himself.

"I don't like talking about my family," he states, the weight of his words hanging heavily in the air. His voice is low, almost a whisper, as if he's already regretting the decision to let me inside these walls. "The town's got enough stories about us. They don't need more."

"I'm not asking for stories, Wade," I reply gently, trying to bridge the gap between us. "Just the history. The truth. You don't have to tell me anything you don't want to. But I think people would appreciate hearing about your family, the real story—not the rumors that swirl like leaves in the wind."

His eyes flicker for a moment, as if he's weighing the decision, yet the wall between us remains unyielding. "Why do you care?" he asks, the edge in his voice sharp enough to slice through the tension.

The question catches me off guard, and I pause before answering, searching for the right words to convey my sincerity. "Because I think the truth matters. And because... I feel like you've been carrying this weight for far too long. I don't know what happened to you, Wade, but I can see it etched on your face, the way it's hurting you. And I genuinely don't think you should have to carry that burden alone."

He stares at me for what feels like an eternity, his jaw tight, his fists clenched so tightly on the table that his knuckles turn white. I can feel the palpable tension in the air, thick and suffocating, as if he's locked in a fierce internal battle, deciding whether to push me away again or finally let me in.

Finally, he exhales a shaky breath, his shoulders slumping slightly in resignation. "Fine. I'll help with the historical details. But that's it. No personal stories, no digging up the past."

A wave of relief washes over me, almost overpowering in its intensity, and I can't help the small smile that tugs at my lips, a flicker of hope igniting within me. "That's all I'm asking for. Thank you."

Wade leans back in his chair, his eyes flicking away from mine for a moment. The silence between us is heavy but not uncomfortable. I can see glimpses of something in him—something kind, something vulnerable—but it's buried deep beneath layers of hurt.

As we sit there, talking about the town's history, I start to see the real Wade, the one who isn't just a man hiding from the world. He's scarred, yes, but there's more to him. There's kindness in the way he talks about his family, even if he tries to keep his voice cold. There's a flicker of something in his eyes when he speaks about the past, like he still cares, even though he doesn't want to admit it.

By the time I leave, Wade has agreed to help me with the Halloween Bash, but I suspect he only offers out of kindness. I take him up on it anyway, because I'd be a fool to turn down his help.

I can feel a connection forming between us, something fragile but real. I don't know where this will lead, but I can't help but hope that, with time, he'll let me in.

CHAPTER 6

Wade

I CAN'T BELIEVE I agreed to help Scarlett with this tour.

I've spent years avoiding anything to do with the town's history, keeping my distance from the gossip and the stories. They all talk like they know me, know my family's legacy. The Grayson name carries too much weight in Buttercup Bay, and I've done everything I can to stay away from it. So, the fact that I'm now helping Scarlett put together a haunted history tour feels like I've lost my damn mind.

But then, there was something in the way she looked at me—it's hard to put into words.

Compassion, understanding—but not pity. She didn't look at me like I was broken or shattered beyond repair. That's what made it impossible to say no, to turn away from her request. It's as if she saw me clearly, not through the fog of my past but as a person capable of moving forward.

Still, I can't shake the dread that clings to me like a second skin, the anxiety that comes with being dragged back into this world I tried so hard to escape. It's not just the stories about my family that I've spent years trying to bury deep within the recesses of my mind, but the town itself, with its familiar streets and haunting memories. Being around people again, being in places where Charlotte and I once wandered hand in hand—it stirs things up, raw emotions that I'm not ready to confront. Those memories, both sweet and painful, bubble to the surface, uninvited and relentless.

But Scarlett... she's different from anyone I've encountered in a long time. There's a light in her that feels impossible to ignore, a warmth that draws me in despite my reservations. And no matter how hard I try to keep my distance, I feel myself softening around her like the edges of my defenses are slowly melting away. She fills the silences with ease, her words flowing effortlessly as she talks about her dreams for the bookstore, her excitement about moving to Buttercup Bay, and the vibrant plans she has for the Halloween Bash. I can't help but admire her tenacity. She's determined, strong, but there's a softness to her too, a kind of quiet courage that resonates deeply within me. I see it in the way she listens, truly listens, and in the way she pushes forward without bulldozing me, always careful, always gentle, as if she understands the fragility of the ground beneath our feet.

As we work together, I find myself letting my guard down, bit by bit. It terrifies me, this vulnerability creeping in like fog on a chilly morning.

We meet every few days to go over the tour details, and each time, I share what I can about the town's rich history, carefully avoiding anything too personal or revealing. I keep Charlotte out of it, firmly drawing a line in the sand. I can't go there—not with Scarlett. Not with anyone. But even though I hold parts of myself back, I feel the connection between us growing stronger with every passing day, like an undercurrent pulling me toward her. I catch myself watching her when she talks, mesmerized by the way her face lights up, her eyes sparkling with enthusiasm when she's passionate about something. I've never met anyone quite like her, and that's the problem.

The more time I spend with her, the harder it is to remember why I built these walls in the first place. Each laugh we share, each shared glance, chips away at my defenses. The pull between us is undeniable, a magnetic force drawing me closer, and it scares the hell out of me. I can't afford to let her get too close; the thought of it sends shivers down my spine. I can't afford to lose someone again—not when the memories of past heartaches still haunt me like shadows in the night.

But tonight, I slip, allowing my guard to falter. We've spent the entire day meticulously poring over the details for the tour, our voices mingling with the fading light of the evening. As the hours stretch into the night, it's well past the time when I should have wrapped things up. Scarlett gathers her things with a grace that captivates me, and before I can think better of it, the words tumble out of my mouth: "I'll walk you home."

She looks up at me, her smile illuminating the dim room like a beacon, and something tightens in my chest—a mixture of warmth and dread. "Thanks, Wade. That's sweet of you," she replies, her voice soft yet laced with an unmistakable warmth that makes my heart race.

I shrug, trying to play it off, but my heart's beating faster than it should be. As we walk through the quiet streets, I find myself hyper-aware of everything—how close she's walking next to me, the sound of her voice as she talks about her favorite books, the way the cool autumn breeze stirs the leaves around us. The town is different at night. Quieter, more intimate. There's something in the air, something that makes the space between us feel heavier.

I listen to Scarlett talk, but my mind is somewhere else entirely. With each step, the tension between us builds, and I can't seem to stop it. I'm caught between wanting to stay right where I am—beside her—and the urge to run back to the safety of my cabin.

When we reach her door, she turns to me, her eyes soft in the dim light. For a moment, neither of us says anything. The air between us feels thick, charged with something unspoken. Scarlett looks up at me, her lips parting slightly as if she's waiting for me to say something. Do something.

I take a step closer without thinking, drawn by an undeniable gravity. Her gaze holds steady, unwavering, and my heart pounds in my chest, a frantic drumbeat that echoes in the silence. Everything in me is screaming to pull her closer, to close the space that feels electric between us. I can feel the pull, like an invisible force drawing me in, urging me to give in to this moment. My hand twitches at my side, as if it has a mind of its own, yearning to reach for her. I lean in just enough that our breaths mingle, a delicate exchange that seems to suspend time itself.

For a second, it feels like the world stills around us, as if the universe is holding its breath, allowing for the possibility that maybe, just maybe, I could take that fateful step forward. But then, the fear crashes into me like a wall, hard and unyielding, shattering the fragile calm. The memory of loss—the haunting image of Charlotte—wraps around my chest, squeezing tight as if to remind me of the stakes. The thought of losing someone again, of allowing myself to let Scarlett in only to watch her slip away like sand through my fingers—it's too much to bear.

I pull back before I can let myself fall any further, the instinct to retreat overpowering the urge to stay.

Scarlett's face shifts, a flicker of hurt crossing her features, and it strikes me like a physical blow. She doesn't say anything, but it's there, clear as day— the disappointment etched into her delicate features. She was expecting something from me, a connection, a moment that I couldn't bring myself to offer.

"I should go," I mumble, stepping away from her door, my voice barely above a whisper. The words feel clumsy, forced, as though they're a confession of my own inadequacy. "Goodnight, Scarlett."

She nods, but there's a sadness in her eyes now, a depth of emotion that pulls at my heartstrings. "Goodnight, Wade," she replies, her voice carrying an unspoken weight that lingers in the air between us.

I turn and walk away, my heart pounding in my ears like a frantic drumbeat. I don't look back, but I can feel her gaze piercing through the darkness, watching me as I retreat into the night, desperate to put as much distance as I can between us. Each step away from her feels heavier than the last, like I'm walking uphill with a weight strapped to my back, a burden of regret and fear that threatens to crush me under its relentless pressure.

By the time I finally make it back to my cabin, frustration bubbles over, and I'm cursing myself, my thoughts spiraling into a chaotic whirlwind. I'm cursing the way I let things get too close, letting a fragile connection form when I should have kept my distance. I'm cursing the way I felt something for the first time in years—an emotion I had sworn to myself I'd never allow to surface again, a promise that now feels like a cruel joke.

I toss my jacket carelessly over the back of a chair, the familiar fabric landing with a soft thud, and I sink down onto the worn floorboards by the fire, its flickering glow casting dancing shadows on the walls. Yet, the warmth of the flames does nothing to thaw the cold knot that has taken residence in my chest, a chilling reminder of the vulnerability I've tried so hard to bury. I close my eyes tightly, attempting to block out the haunting image of Scarlett standing at her door, the hurt reflected in her eyes when I pulled away, a look that feels etched into my mind.

I can't do this. I can't let her in, can't risk the possibility of being hurt again. But even as I desperately tell myself that, deep down, I know it's already too late.

CHAPTER 7

Scarlett

I CAN'T STOP THINKING about that moment at my door. The way Wade leaned in, his breath mingling with mine, created an electric tension that hung thick in the air. The weight of unspoken words lingered between us, heavy and palpable. For a brief second, I thought he was going to kiss me, that our lips would meet in a collision of unfiltered longing. I could feel it in the way his gaze softened, the way his hand hovered just inches from my face, as if he wanted to reach out but couldn't bring himself to cross that final threshold.

But then, in an instant, he pulled away.

It's maddening, this constant torment of knowing there's something undeniable between us, yet feeling like I'm chasing after a ghost that slips through my fingers. One minute, he's there, full of promise and possibility, and the next, he's vanished, retreating back into the shadows of his own mind, leaving me standing alone, adrift in a sea of confusion, wondering what I did wrong to cause such distance. I try not to take it personally, but it's nearly impossible not to when he keeps shutting me out, closing the door on the connection we could have shared, leaving only silence in its wake.

Frustration gnaws at me as I sit in The Lit Lantern, surrounded by a chaotic array of lists and vibrant decorations for the upcoming Halloween Bash. The event is just around the corner, and I'm determined to make it a success, even if Wade seems intent on keeping his distance, like a phantom haunting the edges of my mind. I should be focused on the preparations, meticulously organizing every detail, but my thoughts keep drifting back to him—his rugged handsomeness that could make anyone weak in the knees, the way his eyes softened when we talked, revealing layers of warmth and vulnerability, and the sadness that seemed to linger just beneath the surface, a quiet storm waiting to erupt.

I let out a heavy sigh, rubbing my temples in an attempt to dispel the mounting tension. I need to pull myself together. The town is counting on this event, and I've invested too much time and energy to allow my emotions to cloud my judgment now. Still, it's hard to shake the feeling of confusion that wraps around me like a thick fog, the emotional whiplash of being pulled close one moment and then pushed away the next, leaving me reeling and unsure of where I stand.

"Penny for your thoughts?"

I look up, startled, to see Martha standing in the doorway, her usual basket of freshly baked goods perched on her hip. She walks over with her characteristic grace and sets the basket on the counter, the comforting aroma of warm pastries wafting through the air. Her knowing smile, bright and encouraging, cuts through my haze of distraction. "You look distracted, darling," she observes, her tone inviting me to share the weight of my thoughts with her.

I force a smile, attempting to mask the turmoil churning within me like a storm at sea. "Just thinking about the Bash. Lots to do," I reply, hoping to deflect her curiosity.

Martha narrows her eyes, her expression skeptical and knowing, as if she can see right through my façade. "Uh-huh. And who, exactly, is occupying that pretty head of yours? Because it doesn't look like you're mulling over pumpkins and decorations." Her voice is playful yet probing, urging me to reveal what lies beneath the surface.

With a sigh, I lean back in my chair, the wood creaking slightly under my weight. There's no point in hiding my thoughts from her; she has a way of unearthing the truth. "It's Wade," I admit, the name slipping from my lips like a secret I've been holding too long.

Martha raises an eyebrow, a knowing smile creeping onto her face. "Ah, I thought as much. He has that effect on people, doesn't he? One minute, he's there, and the next, he's gone, like a whisper on the wind." Her voice is laced with understanding, as if she's seen this play out before.

"Exactly," I say, feeling the frustration rise in my chest, tightening like a vice. "He keeps pulling away, and I don't know why. I can feel that there's something real between us, something electric, but every time we get close, he shuts me out. It's like... it's like I'm chasing after someone who doesn't want to be caught, and I can't help but wonder if I'm running in circles for nothing."

Martha nods, her expression softening. "He's been through a lot, Scarlett. You know that. It's not that he doesn't care—he's just... afraid."

"Afraid of what?" I ask, my voice edged with frustration. "Of getting hurt? Of losing someone again? I get that, I really do, but he won't even give me a chance. How am I supposed to help him if he won't let me in?"

Martha reaches across the counter, placing a hand over mine. "You can't force him, darling. But you also can't give up on him. He needs someone who's willing to be patient, who won't walk away the moment things get hard."

I sigh deeply, feeling the weight of her words settle over me like a heavy blanket. "What if he never lets me in? What if I'm just wasting my time? What if all my efforts are in vain, and I end up only hurting myself in the process?"

Martha gives me a gentle smile, one that carries both warmth and understanding. "Then at least you'll know you tried, Scarlett. You'll have the peace of mind that comes with knowing you didn't shy away from the challenge. But something tells me Wade isn't as closed off as he wants people to think. There's a flicker of hope in him, I can feel it. Just... give him time."

I nod slowly, though doubt still lingers like an unwelcome guest in the back of my mind. I don't know how much more time I can give him. I've already let myself fall too far into this emotional whirlpool, and I'm not sure I can handle the hurt if he keeps pulling away, like waves retreating from the shore, leaving me stranded.

But as I sit there, lost in thought about Wade and all the walls he's built around himself—walls that seem impenetrable—I realize something important. I can't keep waiting for him to make the first move. If I'm going to understand why he keeps pushing me away, I need to confront him directly, to break through the barriers he's erected. I need to be brave enough to take that leap, no matter how terrifying it feels.

THE DRIVE UP to Wade's cabin feels longer than usual, the narrow, winding road stretching out before me like a test of my resolve, each twist and turn amplifying the anxiety coiling in my stomach. The trees close in around me, their branches heavy with the weight of autumn's last breath, their vibrant leaves swirling in hues of gold and crimson, a stark contrast to the turmoil within me. It's beautiful up here, serene and quiet, but today the silence feels heavy, as if the world is holding its breath in anticipation of what's to come.

By the time I reach his cabin, my heart is racing, a relentless drumbeat that matches the rush of thoughts swirling in my mind. I don't know what I'm going to say, how I'll articulate the whirlwind of emotions that have been building inside me, but I know I can't leave without answers. I need to understand why he keeps pulling away, why he's so afraid of letting me in, why every step forward feels like two steps back.

I park the car and step out, the crisp air biting at my cheeks, my feet crunching over the brittle leaves scattered across the ground as I make my way to the front door. The familiar scent of pine and earth fills my lungs, grounding me even as my nerves flutter. Before I can knock, Wade opens the door, his expression unreadable, a mask that conceals whatever thoughts may be churning behind those deep-set eyes.

"Scarlett," he says, his voice low, almost a whisper, yet it carries an intensity that sends a shiver down my spine. "What are you doing here?"

I take a deep breath, gathering every ounce of courage I have, forcing myself to meet his gaze, to not shy away from the weight of his question. "I needed to talk to you," I reply, my voice steadier than I feel, each word an invitation to bridge the distance that has grown between us.

His eyes flicker, but he steps aside, letting me in. I walk past him, feeling the tension in the air, thick and heavy. His cabin feels the same—quiet, closed off, like a place where emotions come to die.

I turn to face him, the rhythm of my heart pounding in my chest like a war drum. "Why do you keep pulling away?" I ask, my voice trembling with a mix of frustration and desperation.

Wade stiffens at my words, his jaw tightening, a muscle twitching in his cheek as if he's bracing himself for a blow. "I don't know what you're talking about," he replies, his tone clipped and defensive as if my question has caught him off guard.

"Don't," I say, my voice firmer than I expected, cutting through the tension like a knife. "Don't pretend you don't feel it, too. Every time we get close, you shut me out. You push me away, and I don't understand why. I can't keep doing this, Wade. I need to know what's going on." The words spill out, each one a plea, a desperate attempt to pull him back from the brink of isolation he's created.

He doesn't say anything for a moment, the silence stretching between us like an unbridgeable chasm. His eyes darken, shadows flickering across his face as he looks away, avoiding my gaze as if it were a painful truth. "It's complicated," he finally mutters, the weight of his words heavy in the air.

I let out a frustrated laugh, the sound almost bitter. "Of course it is. But you're not even giving me a chance to understand. You're shutting me out before I can even try." My voice wavers slightly, the edge of exasperation mingling with an aching hope that he might let me in.

Wade's face hardens at my words, the familiar walls coming up again, brick by brick. "You don't understand. You don't know what I've been through." His voice is low, almost a growl, as if he's guarding a secret too painful to share.

"Then tell me!" I plead, stepping closer, my heart pounding with a mix of desperation and determination. "I'm not asking you to bare your soul, but give me something. Anything. I want to help you, Wade, but I can't do that if you keep pushing me away." My words hang between us, a fragile bridge reaching out into the chasm of his silence.

For a moment, I think he's going to say something, that he's finally going to let me in, to share a piece of the burden he carries. But then, just like every time before, he shuts down. His eyes go cold, a storm brewing in their depths, and his expression becomes a fortress—impenetrable and unyielding.

"I can't," he says quietly, each word laden with weight. "I can't do this."

The words hit me like a punch to the gut, knocking the wind from my lungs, and for a moment, I can't breathe. I don't know what I was expecting, but it wasn't this crushing finality. I feel the sting of rejection wash over me, sharp and painful, like icy fingers gripping my heart.

"Fine," I say, my voice barely above a whisper, thick with unshed emotions. "If that's how you want it."

I turn and walk toward the door, each step feeling like a weight dragging me down into an abyss of despair. I don't look back as I leave; I can't. Not when I feel like I've hit a wall I'll never be able to break through, a barrier that looms larger and more daunting with every passing second.

I'VE NEVER FELT MORE TRAPPED.

Scarlett's words echo in my head over and over, refusing to let me rest. *Why do you keep pulling away?* She's right—I am pulling away. But I have to. There's no other way. Letting her in would only mean losing her, and I can't bear the thought of going through that again. The memory of losing Charlotte is burned into me, searing every part of my mind and soul like a brand that refuses to fade.

I stare at the empty cabin, the fire casting flickering shadows across the walls, creating a dance of light and dark that feels almost alive. The silence envelops me—it's quiet, too quiet, as if the world outside has paused to respect my turmoil. Scarlett's laughter still echoes in the corners of my mind, a sweet melody that once filled the silence so easily, like she didn't even notice the heavy weight I carried on my shoulders. But I notice it. Every single day, it presses down on me, a constant reminder of what I'm trying to avoid.

I push the thought of her aside, forcing myself to focus, and turn to the carving on the table, hoping the familiar feel of the wood beneath my fingers and the steady rhythm of my hands will clear my head. The sharp edge of the knife bites into the soft wood, creating smooth, delicate curves that seem to take on a life of their own. Yet, even as I work, my thoughts drift back to her, uninvited. I can't shake the image of the way her eyes softened when she looked at me, the brightness of her gaze piercing through the fog of my despair, or the way her smile tugged at something deep inside me, a long-buried feeling I'd forgotten how to embrace.

I glance down at the carving, and my stomach twists in a way that feels all too familiar. Scarlett. The figure in my hands is undeniably her—delicate and graceful, with her hair flowing in soft, lustrous waves that capture the light just right, her features etched with a gentleness that seems to transcend the wood itself, a quality I can't seem to let go of, no matter how hard I try.

I didn't mean to carve her. I didn't intend to immortalize her likeness in something that's become my refuge, my way of escaping from a world that often feels overwhelming and hostile, a world I keep at arm's length. But here she is, staring back at me with those ethereal eyes, a poignant reminder of everything I'm too afraid to pursue, the dreams I bury beneath layers of self-doubt and fear.

I set the carving down, my hands shaking as if they possess a will of their own. I can't keep doing this—letting her get close, feeling the warmth of her presence, only to push her away when it matters most. But what other choice do I have? The thought of losing her entirely, of letting her in only to watch her slip through my fingers like Charlotte did... it sends a chill through me that feels unbearable, a weight I can't seem to shake.

I stand abruptly, knocking the chair back with a loud scrape that echoes in the stillness. The cabin feels too small, too claustrophobic, closing in on me like a vice, and I desperately need air to fill my lungs. I grab my jacket, feeling the fabric brush against my skin, and step outside into the cool night air, which bites at my skin with a sharpness that is both refreshing and numbing. The trees rustle softly around me, their leaves whispering secrets, the quiet murmur of the wind the only sound accompanying me as I walk through the woods. But even out here, where the vastness of the night sky and the twinkling stars should offer solace, Scarlett's face lingers in my mind, an indelible mark I can't erase, a beacon of what could be or what should never be.

I can't lose her. But if I let her in, it's only a matter of time before I do. The thought sends a shiver down my spine, a warning that echoes in the depths of my mind.

I push forward, my feet carrying me through the woods, deeper into the darkness, trying to outrun the persistent thoughts that won't stop. Each step feels like an exercise in futility, the shadows stretching around me, whispering secrets I can't quite grasp. But it's no use. The more I try to push her away, the stronger the pull becomes, like a tide I can't resist. Her smile, her laughter—they haunt me, swirling like the ghost of something I want but can't have, a haunting melody that lingers in the air long after the music has stopped.

I stop by a tree, its rough bark pressing against my back as I lean against it, closing my eyes in a desperate bid to find some semblance of peace. The guilt is suffocating, wrapping around me like a heavy shroud, pressing down on me like a weight I can't shake off. Charlotte's face flashes in my mind, her bright eyes filled with life, and I can't help but think—if I hadn't led her up that mountain, she'd still be here. Alive. With me. The thought is a sharp blade, cutting deeper with every passing moment.

Scarlett doesn't deserve this. She doesn't deserve to be pulled into the wreckage of my past, into the guilt that keeps me chained to it, a prisoner of my own making. I've been telling myself that pushing her away is the right thing to do, that it's better for her if I keep my distance. But the truth is, it's tearing me apart inside, the internal struggle ripping at the seams of my heart.

I make my way back to the cabin, the silence heavy around me, enveloping me like a dark cloak. The carving of Scarlett sits on the table, unfinished, a testament to my fears and regrets. I pick it up, running my thumb over the smooth surface of her face, tracing the lines of her hair, memorizing the gentle curve of her smile. It's everything I'm too afraid to pursue—everything I've convinced myself I don't deserve, a reflection of the happiness I've buried deep within.

I set the carving aside, a bittersweet ache settling in my chest, knowing I'll never have the courage to give it to her. The weight of unspoken words hangs in the air, heavy with the promise of what might have been, and I can only hope that one day, I'll find the strength to face the truth.

THE DAYS LEADING up to the Halloween Bash are quieter than usual, a stillness that wraps around me like a thick fog. I've been isolating myself, retreating further into the shadows of my own thoughts, avoiding town, avoiding anything that might remind me of Scarlett. Yet, no matter how much distance I try to put between us, her image lingers in my mind like a haunting melody, refusing to fade away.

One afternoon, as I'm chopping wood outside the cabin, the rhythmic thud of the axe against the log is interrupted by the crunch of footsteps on the gravel road behind me. I pause, glancing over my shoulder to see Sheriff Cooper approaching, his face set in that familiar no-nonsense expression he wears so well, a mask of authority that commands respect.

"Wade," he greets me, his voice low but steady, cutting through the stillness like a knife. "Got a minute?"

I nod, wiping the sweat from my forehead with the back of my hand as I lean the axe against a nearby tree, its sharp edge glinting in the sunlight. Cooper crosses his arms over his chest, his posture firm and unwavering, studying me with a gaze that feels both probing and concerned, as if he's trying to figure out the right way to start a conversation that I'm clearly avoiding.

"You've been keeping to yourself more than usual," he states after a long, contemplative pause, his tone serious. "I know you're not one for socializing, but this? This is different. You're isolating yourself."

I shrug, trying to play it off as nonchalantly as I can, though I can feel the weight of his scrutiny. "Just busy. Got a lot to take care of." The words feel hollow, even to me, but I hope he buys it.

Cooper shakes his head, his gaze unwavering and intense, as if trying to pierce through the walls I've built around myself. "No, Wade. It's more than that. You're running from something. Or someone. Scarlett, perhaps."

The mention of Scarlett hits me hard, an unexpected jolt of emotion coursing through me, and I tense involuntarily, my jaw tightening as I struggle to maintain my composure. "I'm not running," I reply, though the words feel weak even as they leave my lips.

"Yes, you are," Cooper counters, his voice firm yet not unkind, like a gentle reminder wrapped in concern. "And we both know why. It's Charlotte."

I stiffen at the sound of her name, a name I haven't heard spoken aloud in what feels like ages. It lingers in the air, heavy and charged, and hearing it now feels like a punch to the gut, a reminder of everything I've tried to bury and forget.

Cooper steps closer, the distance between us shrinking as his voice softens, the concern in his eyes palpable. "Wade, you can't keep punishing yourself for what happened. It wasn't your fault."

"You don't know that," I mutter, my voice barely above a whisper, as my hands clench into fists, the anger and denial swirling within me like a tempest. "If I hadn't taken her up there—"

"Stop," Cooper interrupts, his voice sharp. "You can't keep living like this, blaming yourself for something you couldn't control. Charlotte wouldn't want this for you. She wouldn't want you to shut yourself off from the world, to push people away because you're too afraid to live again."

I grit my teeth, the guilt rising in my throat like bile, a bitter reminder of my past choices. "You don't know what it's like," I manage to say, the weight of my emotions thick in the air between us.

"No, I don't," Cooper admits, his voice steady and unwavering, a calm amidst the storm of my turmoil. "But I do know that you're about to lose something good because you're too wrapped up in the past to see what's right in front of you." His words pierce through the haze of my self-recrimination, striking a nerve I didn't even realize was exposed.

The impact of his statement hits me like a sledgehammer, reverberating in my chest. I know he's talking about Scarlett, and the truth of it cuts deep, slicing through the defenses I've built around my heart. I've been so focused on pushing her away, on creating walls to shield myself from the pain of potential loss, that I didn't realize I'm already losing her, inch by agonizing inch.

Cooper claps a hand on my shoulder, his grip firm and reassuring, grounding me in this moment. "You've got a second chance, Wade. Don't waste it." His sincerity radiates from him, and I feel the weight of his encouragement pressing down on me.

I stand there in silence, his words sinking in like stones thrown into still water, rippling through the depths of my mind. Deep down, I know he's right. I've been hiding behind my guilt for too long, letting it dictate every choice I make, every interaction I avoid. But Scarlett... she's different. She's worth the risk, and I can't let my fears rob me of what could be the best thing to ever happen to me.

Cooper gives me a final nod before turning to leave, his footsteps fading into the distance. I stand there for a long time, staring at the carving of Scarlett on the table, knowing that if I don't make a change soon, I'm going to lose her for good.

And this time, it'll be my fault.

Scarlett

THE TOWN SQUARE is alive with laughter, the soft glow of twinkling lights casting everything in a golden hue that feels almost magical. Pumpkins line the cobblestone paths, their carved faces flickering with candlelight, creating an enchanting display that dances in the evening breeze. The crisp autumn air hums with excitement, filled with the sounds of children playing and adults chatting, all wrapped up in the festive spirit. The *Halloween Bash* is in full swing, a celebration that should have lifted my spirits, yet I find myself feeling hollow inside, unable to fully immerse myself in the revelry around me.

The haunted history tour was a remarkable success, and it seems the town is still buzzing about the spooky stories I pulled together—tales of the town's eerie past, ghostly figures that linger in the nearby woods, and the tragic history that gives Buttercup Bay its haunting charm. I smile and nod as the townspeople approach to congratulate me, their faces glowing with enthusiasm as they thank me for coming out tonight. I respond graciously, but there's an emptiness that lingers beneath my polite demeanor. I can't seem to summon the joy I thought this night would bring, no matter how hard I try.

Because Wade isn't here.

I hadn't admitted it to myself before, but I had hoped—*no*, I had expected—he would show up. Part of me had vividly pictured it: Wade stepping out from the shadows, his rugged form framed by the pumpkins and twinkling lights, a striking figure against the backdrop of festive decorations. I imagined his eyes searching for mine across the crowd, a connection that would spark a flicker of warmth in my heart. He'd come over, maybe smile that rare smile of his that seemed to light up the darkest corners of my world, and...

But he's not here. He didn't come. The thought

settles heavily in my chest, a weight that dulls the vibrant atmosphere around me.

The sharp ache in my chest intensifies as the night drags on. I go through the motions, forcing a smile for the guests, nodding and laughing in all the right places. But none of it feels real. I can't stop thinking about him—about the way he pulled back that night, leaving me standing at my door, feeling more alone than I'd ever felt before. It's not just his absence tonight that hurts—it's everything. The way he keeps pulling away, shutting me out, leaving me guessing whether I'll ever truly reach him.

I should know better. I've been telling myself all night that I'm better off without him—that Wade is too closed off to ever give me what I need. But deep down, I know that's not true. I've already fallen for him, and the thought of walking away feels impossible.

I stand near the corner of the square, watching the last group of guests walk through the pumpkin-lined path. The laughter and chatter fade into the distance, and for a moment, I'm left with nothing but the sound of the wind rustling through the trees. I try to shake the heaviness that's settled over me, but it clings to me like a shadow.

"Scarlett?"

I turn to see Martha walking toward me, her face soft with genuine concern. She wraps me in a warm hug the moment she reaches me, her familiar scent of cinnamon and sugar enveloping me like a comforting blanket on a chilly evening.

"Hey, sweetheart," she says gently, pulling back to meet my gaze. "You did an amazing job tonight. The event was a huge success."

"Thanks," I reply, trying to muster a smile, but it feels brittle and doesn't quite reach my eyes. Martha, with her keen intuition, notices the facade I'm putting on, of course.

"You've been distracted all night," she observes, her voice soft yet probing, like a gentle nudge toward the truth. "Something's on your mind, and I have a feeling I know what—or should I say *who*—it is."

I let out a heavy sigh, rubbing my hands together against the chill that lingers in the air, a stark contrast to the warmth of the gathering earlier. "It's Wade. He didn't come." There's a weight to my words, as if the very mention of his name pulls me further into the shadows that have been clinging to me all evening.

Martha nods, her expression calm and knowing, as if she'd anticipated that answer all along. "I figured that might be the case; it's not surprising, really."

"I thought... I thought maybe he'd show up," I admit, my voice catching in my throat, the weight of hope slowly deflating. "I guess I was wrong." The disappointment hangs heavily in the air, a palpable reminder of my expectations.

Martha steps closer, her gaze warm and understanding, radiating a quiet strength that seems to envelop me. "You know Wade isn't the easiest man to reach. He's been through a lot, and he's built some pretty strong walls around himself. It's like he's constructed a fortress, and only he has the key."

"I know," I say, frustration rising in my chest like a tide threatening to overwhelm me. "But it's like I keep trying and trying, and every time we get close, he pulls away. I don't know what else I can do. I feel like I'm chasing after someone who doesn't even want to be caught." My voice grows softer, tinged with a sense of helplessness, as I grapple with the reality of my situation.

Martha's eyes soften, and she places a hand on my arm. "Sometimes love isn't easy, Scarlett. Sometimes, it takes a lot of patience and a lot of heart. Wade... he's not like most men. He's carrying a heavy burden, and it's going to take time for him to let someone in."

"I don't know if I have any fight left in me," I confess, my voice breaking slightly. "I've been giving everything I have, but I can't keep doing this if he's just going to keep pushing me away. I feel like I'm standing out in the cold, waiting for him to let me in, and he won't."

Martha's hand squeezes mine gently, her warmth a comforting presence amidst my turmoil. "I know, darling. I know it's hard. But Wade is worth fighting for. He just needs someone who's willing to stay, even when things get tough. Someone like you."

I blink back the sting of tears, shaking my head in despair. "What if I'm not that person? What if I'm not strong enough for that? What if I just don't have it in me to be there for him when he needs it most?" The weight of my uncertainty hangs heavily in the air, pressing down on my chest.

Martha gives me a sad smile, her eyes reflecting a depth of understanding. "Only you can answer that, Scarlett. But don't walk away just because it's hard. Sometimes the best things in life are the ones we have to fight for, the ones that demand our courage and our devotion." Her words resonate within me, a bittersweet melody that both comforts and challenges.

Her words hang in the air between us, lingering like an unspoken promise. For a moment, I don't know what to say, the silence stretching out like an unwelcome visitor. I want to believe that Wade is worth the fight—that he'll come around, that he'll finally let me in and share the burdens he's been carrying alone. But I'm tired. I'm so tired of waiting, of hoping, of feeling like I'm standing on the precipice of something beautiful yet unattainable, something that's never going to happen. The thought wraps around me like a cold shroud, and I wonder if I have the strength to keep fighting.

As the night begins to wind down, I watch the last of the guests leave the square, their laughter fading into the distance. The twinkling lights still glow warmly against the dark sky, but the festive atmosphere feels far away now, as if I'm watching it from the outside.

I glance around one last time, my heart clinging to a thread of hope—just hoping—that maybe, somehow, Wade will suddenly appear in the crowd, with that familiar smile lighting up his face. But he doesn't. The space where he should be remains empty, an aching reminder of what I long for.

Martha wraps her arms around me once more before she leaves, her warmth enveloping me in a comforting embrace. She whispers, "You're stronger than you think, Scarlett. Don't forget that." Her words linger in the air, a fragile balm for my frayed spirit.

I nod in response, though uncertainty gnaws at me. Standing there, isolated amidst the fading remnants of the celebration, I watch the pumpkins flicker their last light and the leaves swirl playfully in the chill of the breeze. With each passing moment, the hollow feeling in my chest deepens, echoing the quiet of the night. This evening should have been a triumph, a monumental moment to celebrate all my hard work and dedication. But instead, it feels like a poignant goodbye, a farewell to dreams I once cherished.

Wade isn't coming. And as much as it hurts to accept this reality, I know I can't keep waiting for him, not when the world continues to turn around me, urging me to move forward.

CHAPTER 10

Wade

MY HEART POUNDS in my chest as I stand at the edge of the town square, hidden in the shadows. The Halloween Bash is winding down, and I can hear the soft murmur of voices, the clinking of glasses, and the distant sound of laughter. The whole square is bathed in warm light from the jack-o'-lanterns and string lights hanging overhead. It's the kind of night that should feel comforting, but right now, it feels like a weight pressing down on me.

Every instinct I have is screaming at me to turn back, to leave before anyone notices I'm here. I grip the edge of my jacket, my palms slick with sweat, and I start to take a step back. But Cooper's words keep running through my mind, over and over, like a loop I can't escape.

"You've got a second chance, Wade. Don't waste it."

I swallow hard, my throat dry as I glance toward the square again. I know what I have to do, but the thought of actually doing it makes my hands shake. What if I screw this up? What if it's too late? The idea of losing Scarlett because I was too much of a coward to let her in… I can't let that happen. I can't live with that regret.

I take a deep breath, filling my lungs with the crisp air, and step into the square, my legs trembling as if they might give out at any moment. My eyes scan the thinning crowd, desperately searching for her, and then I see her—standing near her beloved bookstore, alone in a world that feels too vast and empty. Her arms are wrapped around herself, a protective gesture, like she's trying to hold the pieces of her heart together, and the profound sadness etched on her face makes my chest tighten with guilt.

She looks lost. Hurt. And I know I'm the reason for it. I did this to her, and the weight of that realization presses down on me.

My stomach twists in knots as I force myself to walk toward her, each step feeling heavier than the last, as if the ground beneath me is trying to pull me back. The square feels too open, too exposed, like a spotlight shining down on my insecurities. I can't shake the feeling that everyone is watching, their eyes boring into me, but at the same time, it's as if the rest of the world has fallen away, leaving just Scarlett and me suspended in this moment.

She hasn't seen me yet, but when I'm just a few feet away, she turns. Her eyes widen in surprise, a flicker of hope mingled with confusion, and for a moment, we simply stare at each other, caught in an unspoken connection. She doesn't say anything, but I can see the question burning in her gaze, the uncertainty swirling around her like a storm. She's wondering why I'm here, and honestly, so am I. But deep down, I know what I need to do, even if the thought of it scares the hell out of me. The fear gnaws at my insides, but I can't let it hold me back any longer.

Before I can lose my nerve, I step closer and take her hand. Her skin is soft, warm against the cold air, and the touch sends a jolt through me. Scarlett's eyes search mine, her breath catching, but she doesn't pull away.

"Scarlett," I begin, my voice shaking. God, this is harder than I thought. I feel like my whole chest is cracking open, like every emotion I've been holding in is rushing to the surface all at once. "I... I need to tell you something. I've been... I've been an idiot."

She blinks, her eyes widening further, but she stays silent, allowing me the space to pour out my heart.

"I've been pushing you away because I've been scared. Scared of opening up, scared of losing someone again." I pause, my throat tightening as the words I've been holding back for so long finally spill out like a dam breaking. "When Charlotte died, I blamed myself. I thought if I never let anyone get close again, I wouldn't have to feel that kind of pain. I thought I was protecting myself... but all I've done is hurt you."

Scarlett's hand tightens slightly in mine, her grip both reassuring and electrifying, but she still doesn't speak. She's just watching me, her eyes shining with something I can't quite decipher. Hope? Hurt? It's a mix of emotions swirling beneath the surface, and I'm left grappling with the uncertainty of it all.

I take another deep breath, my heart racing as if it's trying to break free from my chest. "The truth is... I care about you, Scarlett. More than I've cared about anyone in a long time. And that terrifies me. But I'm done running. I'm done letting fear control me. I don't want to lose you. I'm willing to take the risk if you'll have me." The weight of my confession hangs in the air between us, a fragile moment suspended in time, and I can only hope she feels the same urgency that grips me.

The words hang in the air between us, and for a moment, I feel as if I can't breathe. My whole world teeters on the edge of this singular moment, and all I can do is wait for her response. I've never been more scared in my life; the adrenaline courses through my veins, amplifying every heartbeat.

Scarlett stares at me, her lips parted slightly, as though she's struggling to process everything I just laid bare before her. The silence stretches on, thick and heavy, and I feel the familiar knot of fear tightening in my chest, squeezing tighter with each passing second. What if I'm too late? What if I've already pushed her too far, and there's no turning back now?

But then, slowly, her expression softens. Her eyes, which had been clouded with confusion and sadness, begin to fill with something else—something warmer, something I haven't seen in what feels like an eternity. A flicker of hope ignites within me, battling against the shadows of doubt.

Without a word, Scarlett steps closer, her movements deliberate and filled with intention, and pulls me into a kiss. The second her lips touch mine, it's as if everything inside me shatters and falls back into place all at once, like a puzzle finally completing its picture. The tension I've been carrying, the fear, the guilt—it all melts away in the warmth and tenderness of her kiss, leaving only the pure, undeniable connection that draws us together.

The square seems to erupt around us, the sounds of applause and cheers crashing like waves against the shore, breaking through the haze that clouds my mind. Yet, none of it matters. None of it registers in my overwhelmed heart. All I can feel is Scarlett, the warmth of her hand gripping mine with a fierce determination, the way her kiss envelops me like a promise I never dared to hope I'd deserve.

When she pulls back, her eyes lock onto mine again, and in that moment, I can see it—the unspoken invitation—she's letting me in, revealing the depths of her heart.

"I'm willing to take the risk too," she whispers, her voice soft but steady, imbued with a resolve that ignites my spirit.

Relief floods through me like a rush of cool water in a parched desert, and I pull her into my arms, holding her tight as the world spins around us in a dizzying dance of sound and light. I never thought I'd get to feel this again—the thrill of connection, the warmth of hope rekindled. I never thought I'd have a second chance at something so beautiful.

But here I am, heart racing and breathless, and I'm not letting go. Not now, not ever.

CHAPTER 11

Scarlett

THE LATE AUTUMN breeze carries the scent of pine and woodsmoke as Wade and I walk hand in hand through the streets of Buttercup Bay. The golden light of the setting sun bathes the town in a soft glow, making everything feel warm and peaceful, even as the air cools. There's a quiet contentment in the way we move together now, no more hesitation or unspoken tension—just the comfort of being with someone who understands me completely.

It's been weeks since Wade stood before the entire town, laying everything bare with an honesty that took my breath away. I can still feel the rush of emotions from that moment, the way his voice trembled with vulnerability as he told me he was ready to take the risk of opening up. Since then, every day has been a testament to his sincerity, as he continues to show me just how deeply he meant it.

Wade has opened up to me in ways I never thought possible, peeling back the layers of his soul like pages in a cherished book. It's not just about him sharing his past anymore—though we've had heartfelt conversations about Charlotte, about the grief that still lingers and the guilt that sometimes shadows him—but it's also the way he shares his present with me. His dreams, those fleeting moments of quiet contemplation, and the little things that make him the man he is today draw me closer to him.

A few days ago, he invited me into his cozy cabin, its walls lined with the scent of aged wood and the faint crackle of a fire. He showed me the wood carvings he'd been diligently working on, and I was completely unprepared for the depth of his talent. His hands, so steady and strong, brought forth delicate, beautiful creations that seemed to breathe with life. When he unveiled the carving of me, my heart nearly stopped.

It was stunning—me, captured in wood, with my hair flowing in soft waves, my expression gentle yet resolute. I could see myself through his eyes in that carving, and it moved me in a way that transcended words, evoking emotions I could hardly articulate.

"I didn't plan on making this," Wade had said quietly, his voice almost shy as he handed it to me with a tenderness that warmed my heart and sent a rush of warmth through my veins. "It just… happened."

I remember staring at it, utterly captivated, running my fingers over the smooth wood, feeling the intricate details beneath my touch, tears prickling my eyes as the weight of his sentiment washed over me. "It's beautiful," I whispered, my voice barely above a breath. "Wade, I… I don't even know what to say."

"You don't have to say anything," he replied, his voice low and soothing, a gentle balm to my overwhelmed heart. "I just wanted you to have it."

The carving is on my nightstand now, a daily reminder of how far we've come, a testament to our shared journey and the bond we've forged through trials and triumphs alike. Each time I catch a glimpse of it, I feel a swell of gratitude for his artistry and the unspoken connection that continues to deepen between us.

As we walk now, I squeeze Wade's hand gently, feeling his warmth seep into me. Buttercup Bay feels more like home than ever, but it's not the bookstore or the cozy town that makes me feel that way. It's Wade. It's the way he's let me in, the way we've healed each other without even realizing it.

I glance over at him, catching the soft look in his eyes as he glances down at me. There's something about the way he looks at me now—like he's not just seeing me, but all the things we've been through together. The walls he built around himself are gone, and in their place is a man who's ready to live again.

"You've been quiet," Wade says, his voice rumbling low, resonating with an earnest curiosity. "What's going on in that head of yours?"

I smile, leaning into him a little as we walk, finding warmth in his presence. "Just thinking about how lucky I am."

His eyebrows lift in surprise, the corner of his mouth tugging into a small, teasing smile that lights up his face. "Oh yeah? What'd I do to deserve that?"

I laugh softly, the sound mingling with the gentle rustle of the leaves beneath our feet, a symphony of nature echoing our shared moment. "You showed me your heart, Wade. That's more than enough."

His hand tightens around mine, a small but profound gesture, and for a moment, we walk in comfortable silence, the world around us fading into the background. I can feel the weight of his gratitude in that simple connection—no words needed to convey what we both understand.

"I've been thinking," I say after a beat, my voice tentative but hopeful, like the first light of dawn breaking through the darkness. "About your carvings."

Wade raises an eyebrow, a mixture of curiosity and hesitation evident in his expression. "What about them?"

"I think you should share them with the town. Show people what you can do." I glance at him, my heart racing slightly as I notice the uncertainty flickering across his face like a candle in the wind.

"You're so talented, Wade. People would love to see your work and appreciate the beauty you create."

He stays quiet for a moment, his gaze fixed ahead, lost in thought as we continue our walk. I can almost see the gears turning in his mind, the idea of stepping out of the shadows and letting people in just a little more weighing heavily on him. It's a lot to ask from someone who has spent so long guarding his passion, but I know deep down he's capable of it.

"I don't know," he says finally, his voice slow and deliberate as if he's still testing the waters of this idea in his mind. "Maybe. I'm not sure if I'm ready for that."

I smile gently, hoping to reassure him in this delicate moment. "There's no rush. I just want people to see what I see in you, the incredible artist waiting to be discovered, like a hidden gem waiting to catch the light."

His gaze softens, and he pulls me a little closer, his warmth brushing against mine as we walk side by side, the world around us fading into a comfortable blur. "You always see the good in me, don't you?

Like you have this magical ability to uncover the best parts of me."

"I do," I say, my voice quiet but firm, each word laced with conviction and sincerity. "Because it's there, waiting to be shared with the world, like a masterpiece yearning to be unveiled to those who will appreciate its beauty."

The sun dips lower in the sky, casting long shadows over the town, and the golden light dances across the pavement, but the warmth between us keeps the encroaching chill at bay. As we stroll past the quaint bookstore, its windows glowing with soft light, I feel a profound sense of peace wash over me. This town, these streets—it's where I belong, where my heart has found its rhythm. But more than that, it's Wade. He's my home now, the anchor in a swiftly changing world.

I never thought I'd find this kind of happiness, not after everything I'd been through, the struggles and heartaches that once felt insurmountable. When I moved to Buttercup Bay, I was searching for a fresh start, a place to call my own, a sanctuary from the past. What I didn't realize was that home isn't just a place—it's the people who make you feel like you belong, who wrap you in warmth and understanding. And Wade? He's that person for me, the one who makes every day feel like a new beginning.

As we stroll past the twinkling lights that adorn the pumpkin-lined streets, I lean my head gently against Wade's shoulder, savoring the comforting rhythm of his steady breath. For the first time in what feels like an eternity, a profound sense of peace washes over me. It's as if the world has faded away, and I'm exactly where I'm meant to be, enveloped in this moment.

Wade tilts his head to press a soft kiss to the crown of my hair, his voice barely above a whisper when he finally breaks the silence. "I'm glad you didn't give up on me."

I close my eyes, allowing a smile to spread across my face as I nestle against the warmth of his jacket, the fabric a shield against the cool evening air. "I couldn't. You're worth it," I reply, my heart swelling with affection.

As we meander through the tranquil town, fingers intertwined, the soft glow of the lights casting a golden hue around us, I realize with certainty—this is our happily ever after, a promise of love and belonging that stretches into the horizon.

ONE YEAR LATER

THE STREETS of Buttercup Bay are dressed in all the colors of autumn again, pumpkins lining the cobblestone paths and twinkling lights strung between the lampposts. The crisp air is filled with the scent of spiced cider and the warmth of freshly baked pies, reminding me of just how much can change in a year. Last Halloween, I was new to this town, uncertain about my place here, and even more uncertain about Wade.

But now, as I stroll through these familiar streets, Wade's hand wrapped securely around mine, everything feels right. Complete. This place isn't just where I live—it's my home, a vibrant tapestry woven with countless memories. And so is he, the anchor in my ever-evolving story.

We walk side by side, the town humming with preparations for this year's Halloween Bash, an event that brings the community together in a delightful swirl of laughter and creativity. I watch as families decorate their shops with colorful banners and twinkling lights, their children darting about in eager excitement, faces painted with joyful anticipation. I can't help but smile, soaking in the atmosphere. It's the same festival, yet this time, I'm not engulfed by the anxiety or uncertainty that clouded my heart a year ago. It's incredible how much peace and love can transform the lens through which you view the world around you, turning familiar sights into cherished treasures.

Wade glances at me, his thumb brushing gently across the back of my hand, a simple gesture that sends warmth coursing through me. "You're quiet," he observes, his voice a deep rumble that always seems to ground me, wrapping me in a sense of security.

"I'm just... happy," I reply, squeezing his hand a little tighter, the connection between us palpable, almost electric. It's a simple gesture, yet it feels monumental, anchoring me in this moment.

"Thinking about how much has changed since last year."

"Yeah," he murmurs, a small smile tugging at the corner of his lips, his eyes sparkling with shared memories and unspoken promises that linger between us like a warm glow. "A lot has changed, and it's all been worth it."

He pauses, and I can tell he's deep in thought, his brow furrowing slightly as he considers his words. Wade has come so far—he doesn't retreat into silence as much as he used to, his voice now a steady presence in my life. Over the past year, he's let me in, little by little, until we've built something beautiful, something that feels as if it'll endure the test of time, like the strongest of bonds.

He stops walking, turning to face me fully, his eyes soft and sincere as they search mine for understanding. "I've been thinking about something," he says, his voice gentle, wrapped in the warmth of anticipation, but there's an edge of excitement there too, an energy that sends a thrill through me.

"Oh?" I tilt my head, curiosity piquing my interest like a gentle nudge. "What's on your mind?" I lean in slightly, eager to hear what thoughts have sparked this newfound enthusiasm in him.

He glances around at the town, taking in the familiar streets that have woven themselves into the fabric of his life, then shifts his gaze toward the majestic mountains rising in the distance, their peaks kissed by the clouds. "I've been thinking about building us a place. A home. Somewhere up near the mountains, close to nature, but still close to the town. Somewhere that's ours, a sanctuary we can retreat to."

My heart skips a beat, warmth spreading through my chest like sunlight breaking through the clouds on a crisp morning. A home. The word carries so much weight now—so much meaning and promise. A year ago, I wouldn't have imagined standing here, wrapped in this moment, hearing Wade talk about building a life together, but now? It feels like the most natural thing in the world, as if it has been destined all along.

I smile up at him, my heart brimming with hope and happiness. "I love that idea," I say softly, my voice infused with affection and sincerity. "A place that's all ours. Somewhere we can build together, filled with laughter and love, where every corner tells our story."

Wade's gaze softens, and for a moment, he just looks at me, the love in his eyes unmistakable. "You're my home, Scarlett," he whispers, his voice rough but full of emotion. "I didn't think I'd ever feel like this again. Like I could let someone in. But you... you made me believe it's possible."

His words hit me straight in the heart, and I blink back the tears that prick at the corners of my eyes. "You've always been worth it," I say, reaching up to cup his cheek. "I'm just glad you saw that too."

We stand there for a moment, wrapped in the quiet of the town as the preparations for the Bash continue around us. There's so much life here, so much warmth, and I realize how much we've both healed in this place. It's not just Buttercup Bay that feels like home—it's Wade. We've built something together that's stronger than anything I could have imagined when I first came here.

As we start walking again, Wade's hand firmly in mine, I look out over the town, my heart swelling with gratitude. I never expected this—moving to Buttercup

Bay was supposed to be a fresh start, a way to rebuild my life after everything that had gone wrong. I thought I'd find comfort in the bookstore, in the quiet charm of a small town, but instead, I found love. I found him.

"I can't wait to see what our future looks like," I say quietly, leaning my head against Wade's shoulder as we walk, feeling the steady rhythm of his steps beside me.

"Neither can I," he replies, his voice full of warmth and certainty, wrapping around me like a cozy blanket. "We'll build something beautiful, Scarlett. You and me. Together."

And as we stroll through the pumpkin-lined streets, the last rays of the autumn sun casting everything in a shimmering gold, I know he's right. Our future —our life together—holds the promise of joy and adventure, something that will surpass even my wildest dreams.

Because for the first time in a long time, I'm exactly where I belong. With him, in this moment that feels so perfectly right.